# Dappled Apples

by JAN CARR

illustrated by

DOROTHY DONOHUE

Holiday House / New York

The text typeface is Kidprint Bold.

The collage artwork was created with handmade cut paper
that was layered and crumpled to achieve texture and dimension.


First Edition

Library of Congress Cataloging-in-Publication Data
Carr, Jan.
Dappled apples / by Jan Carr; illustrated by Dorothy Donohue.—1st ed.
p.  cm.
Summary: Rhyming text and illustrations celebrate the pleasures of fall,
from turning leaves and apple picking to pumpkins and Halloween.
ISBN 0-8234-1583-X
[1. Autumn—Fiction.  2. Stories in rhyme.]  I. Donohue, Dorothy, ill.  II. Title.

PZ8.3.C21687 Dap  2001

[E]—dc21     00-047285

For Gwen, Tom, Nell,
and Kate,
who pick the *best* orchards,
and for Charlie, the apple of my eye
—J. C.


To Mary Jo, for her wit and humor
and to Jerry, for his kind heart and wise mind
—D. D.

Flutter, flitter
Gold as glitter

Colors crackle
Round the tree

Rake a heap up
Run and leap up
Fall is frisky—
So are we!

Tiptoe, teeter
Which one's sweeter?
Dappled apples
Sunny streaks

Saggy branches
Avalanches!
Crunchy, bunchy
Apple cheeks

Tug a tall one
Hug a small one
Lug a fat one
Through the patch

Stack a mile up
Pumpkin pileup
Scarecrows watch
As snitches snatch

Teeth are zigzag
Tail goes wigwag
Seeds are slimy
Scoop the goop

Try a hat on
This, then that on
Time for tricking!
Out we troop

Evil fairy
Yikes! She's scary!
Patched-up pirate
Who is he?

Pup parading?
Masquerading!
Fall'll fool you—

See! It's me!